PRINCESS PULVERIZER

gotta WARN tHe UNiCORNS!

PENGUIN WORKSHOP

An Imprint of Penguin Random House LLC, New York

Text copyright © 2019 by Nancy Krulik. Illustrations and logo copyright © 2019 by
Penguin Random House LLC. All rights reserved. Published by Penguin Workshop,
an imprint of Penguin Random House LLC, New York. PENGUIN and PENGUIN
WORKSHOP are trademarks of Penguin Books Ltd, and the W colophon is a
registered trademark of Penguin Random House LLC. Printed in the USA.

Visit us online at www.penguinrandomhouse.com.

Library of Congress Cataloging-in-Publication Data is available upon request.

ISBN 9781524791568 (pbk)   10 9 8 7 6 5 4 3 2 1
ISBN 9781524791575 (hc)   10 9 8 7 6 5 4 3 2 1

NANCY KRULIK

Princess PULVERIZER

Gotta WARN THE UNICORNS!

art by Ian McGinty
based on original character designs by
Ben Balistreri

Penguin Workshop

For Amanda and Alex, who are mystical and magical,

like unicorns—NK

To all the princesses and princes pulverizing with prowess!

—IM

CHAPTER 1

"Do you know the difference between a unicorn and a carrot? One is a funny beast, and the other is a bunny feast!"

Princess Pulverizer doubled over, laughing at the joke.

Her buddy Lucas laughed along with her. "That's funny," he said.

"There's a whole chapter of unicorn jokes in this book." Princess Pulverizer held up her copy of *Unicorns from A to Z*.

"Here's another one: 'You know why the unicorn didn't join the king's army? He didn't like the *uni*-form.'"

Lucas giggled. But Princess Pulverizer's other friend, Dribble, didn't. So she searched the book for something he might find interesting. "Did you know unicorns change colors to match their surroundings?"

Dribble barely seemed to be listening.

"Here's another fun fact," Lucas added. "Unicorns eat flowers."

"You're right," Princess Pulverizer said. "It's here on page nine."

"I don't need a book," Lucas said. "I'm watching Fortune eat his breakfast."

Princess Pulverizer looked over at the young unicorn they'd been traveling with. He was eating a bed of purple tulips.

"Look! His fur is turning purple!" Lucas
exclaimed.

"Told ya," Princess Pulverizer said as
Fortune pranced toward some bright red
and yellow marigolds. "Now he's red and
yellow."

Fortune took a big bite of marigolds.
Yellow pollen blew into the air.

Aachoooooooo! Dribble sneezed so
hard a flicker of a flame escaped his
mouth. "Grrr . . . allergies," the dragon
complained.

Princess Pulverizer turned to her book.
"What did the baby unicorn say to the
mommy unicorn?"

"What?" Lucas asked.

"Where's my Pop-*corn*?" The princess laughed so hard she snorted.

"We really need to focus on looking for *Fortune's* parents, and his whole herd," Dribble reminded her.

"A unicorn's herd is called a blessing," Princess Pulverizer corrected him.

"It would be a *real* blessing if you would start searching for unicorns," Dribble insisted.

Princess Pulverizer really did want to find Fortune's family. After all, it was her fault he was separated from them. She was the one who'd lured him out of the woods and into plain sight, where he could be captured.

But she hadn't meant to do that. She'd been *tricked* into helping an evil traveling showman named Ralf with his plot to capture a real unicorn.

Ralf was very mean, and very greedy. He'd forced Fortune into a cage, which had made the unicorn miserable. But all Ralf cared about was how much he could charge the people of Beeten Wheeten to come stare at a real live unicorn.

Thanks to some fast thinking and true bravery on Dribble's part, Fortune had been freed. But that didn't change the fact that while Fortune was caged, his entire blessing had disappeared. The princess figured they'd gone out searching for Fortune.

The only way Princess Pulverizer was ever going to be able to forgive herself was to reunite Fortune with his family. That would be a good deed. Perhaps the best Princess Pulverizer had ever accomplished.

Which was saying something, because Princess Pulverizer was an expert at good deeds.

She had to be. Good deeds were what a Quest of Kindness was all about. And the princess had been on just such a quest for quite a while. So far, she and her friends had accomplished six good deeds. Which meant she only had two more to go before her greatest wish could come true. After completing eight good deeds . . . Princess Pulverizer would be allowed to go to Knight School!

The Quest of Kindness had been her father's idea. King Alexander of Empiria loved his daughter, Princess Serena (boy, did Princess Pulverizer hate when he called her that!). But he also believed she was too selfish, spoiled, and snobby to be a knight.

He hoped that by doing good deeds for others, she might become more knightlike.

Oh, and King Alexander had insisted she bring back eight tokens of gratitude from the folks she'd helped as proof she had actually completed her good deeds. Because the princess could also be a bit of a fibber.

"Okay. No more facts or jokes," Princess Pulverizer said. *"For now."*

"Good." Dribble leaned back against a tree and began to scratch a hard-to-reach itch against its bark. "Finding Fortune's . . . hey, where *is* Fortune?" Princess Pulverizer looked around.

The unicorn was nowhere to be seen.

"I thought *you* were keeping track of him," Princess Pulverizer told Dribble. "I was too busy reading from the book to keep my eye on him."

"I was too busy telling you to *stop* reading from the book to look out for him," Dribble answered.

The princess and the dragon both turned to Lucas.

"Don't look at me," he said. "I was too busy laughing at Princess Pulverizer's jokes."

"We'll find him. Easy peasy," Princess Pulverizer assured her friends. She began calling, "Here, Fortune. Here, boy!"

"I'm not sure he even *knows* his name *is* Fortune," Lucas added. "We've only just named him, after all."

That *did* make things a bit more difficult.

"Ow!" Dribble suddenly grabbed his rear end and jumped. "Cut that out!"

"Cut *what* out?" Princess Pulverizer asked.

"You pulled my tail."

"How could I?" the princess argued. "I was standing right here."

"Lucas?" Dribble asked.

"I'd never pull your tail," Lucas assured him.

"Then who?" Dribble looked around.

"M-m-maybe it was a ghost!" Lucas stammered.

"Don't be ridiculous," Princess Pulverizer said. "Dribble must have *imagined* someone pulled on his tail."

"I did not," Dribble insisted.

"Shhh . . ." Lucas interrupted. "Did you hear that?"

Princess Pulverizer listened. Something was definitely rustling behind those bushes and trees.

"We're going in," she declared.

"We don't know what's in there," Lucas said nervously.

"Come on, little buddy," Dribble urged Lucas. "We'll go together. You don't want to stay here alone, do you?"

"I don't like being alone," Lucas admitted.

Princess Pulverizer began making her way through the bushes and trees. "It has to be Fortune. Who else . . . WHOA!" Princess Pulverizer gasped as she walked into a clearing. "What an amazing garden!"

"There's Fortune!" Dribble added excitedly.

"No wonder he came here," Lucas chimed in. "There's a lake to drink from and a whole buffet of blossoms to eat."

"He's really pigging out on those petunias," Princess Pulverizer said. "I'm getting hungry watching him."

"I wouldn't mind a melted swiss cheese on rye," Lucas agreed.

"We're out of rye bread," Dribble replied. "We haven't got any cheese, either."

"I saw a sign for a kingdom a while back," the princess recalled. "Let's go and get supplies."

"We're *supposed* to be looking for unicorns," Dribble reminded her. "Going back to where we came from isn't going to help. Besides, I don't want to risk taking Fortune into a kingdom. Some greedy person might want to capture him again."

That was true. And yet . . .

Grumble rumble! Princess Pulverizer's empty stomach was saying something else.

"What's Fortune doing now?" Lucas pointed toward the edge of the lake. The unicorn was twirling on his hind legs.

"Looks like a happy dance," Princess Pulverizer replied. *"Probably because his belly is full,"* she added, glaring accusingly at Dribble.

"He's awfully close to the water," Lucas noted. "Can unicorns swim?"

"Let's see." Princess Pulverizer opened her copy of *Unicorns from A to Z*.

SPLASH!

Before the princess could find the right chapter, Fortune twirled himself right into the lake.

"I'll save you, Fortune!" Dribble called.

But Fortune didn't *need* saving. The unicorn was dog-paddling—er, *unicorn*-paddling—in the cool clear water. He stopped to snack on some water lilies, then swam back toward shore.

As Fortune climbed out of the water, he

galloped over to Dribble and yanked the dragon's tail with his teeth.

"Ow!" Dribble cried.

"I guess we know who pulled your tail," Princess Pulverizer said, laughing. "Fortune was hiding in the bushes, and he got you."

Fortune shook his body. Water splashed all over Dribble.

"Now I'm soaked," the dragon groaned. "And I've got mud between my toes." He began picking at his feet. "This stuff hardens fast."

"You stay here and dry off," Princess Pulverizer suggested. "Lucas and I will go into the kingdom for supplies."

"Make it fast," Dribble finally agreed. "We're losing daylight. And it won't be easy to go unicorn searching in the dark."

CHAPTER 2

"The king here must be brave," Lucas said as he and Princess Pulverizer entered the kingdom of Leononia. "His royal crest has a lion on it. Lions are brave—like I wish I could be."

Princess Pulverizer didn't respond. There wasn't much she could say without hurting her friend's feelings.

"Come on," she replied instead. "Let's get some food. I'm starving."

"Please make sure that roast beef is lean," the princess heard a woman saying as she walked into a nearby food shop. "It's for the king. I'm his chef."

"You're not the royal chef I met yesterday," the shopkeeper said. "Or the one I met the day before."

"Nobody in the king's kitchen keeps their job very long," the chef admitted.

Princess Pulverizer snickered. *The king must be one picky eater. Why else would he keep firing chefs?*

"The king is convinced that his previous chefs were all trying to poison him," the woman continued.

That is another explanation.

"I need a bag of navy beans, too," the chef continued. "King Harvey wants beans with every meal."

"Don't they give him gas?" the shopkeeper asked her.

"*Terribly*," the chef agreed. "You can't imagine the sounds that come out of that man. Every time his stomach hurts, he fears he's been poisoned," the chef explained.

The shopkeeper laughed. "The king *is* a bit fearful."

"Afraid of his own shadow," the chef added.

"Can't the royal doctor convince the king that it's the beans causing his tummy trouble?" the shopkeeper wondered.

"He doesn't believe him," the chef replied. "King Harvey is convinced the only way to stay safe from poison is to drink from a unicorn's horn. So he has ordered his knights to bring him one."

"Good luck with that. There's no such thing as a unicorn," the shopkeeper scoffed.

Princess Pulverizer opened her mouth to insist that unicorns were very real, and that their horns were called *alicorns*, but before she could get a word out, the chef said something very alarming.

"One of the knights actually spotted one—an old fellow, with little strength."

"That should have made him easy prey," the shopkeeper pointed out. "If he really saw a unicorn, why didn't he catch him?"

"It was before the king gave his order,"

the chef explained. "I'm hoping the knight will find the old unicorn again and present King Harvey with his horn. It's probably the only way I will keep my job past tonight's dinner."

Princess Pulverizer gasped so loudly they both turned to stare at her.

"Can I help you, miss?" the shopkeeper asked.

"Um . . . *no*," the princess answered nervously. She grabbed Lucas by the arm. "Come on. We have to get out of here."

"But we haven't bought anything," Lucas objected.

"We don't have time," the princess argued. "We have to get back. NOW!"

"How am I supposed to make grilled cheese sandwiches without cheese or bread?" Dribble wondered when Princess Pulverizer and Lucas arrived back in the garden empty-handed.

"We can eat later," Princess Pulverizer told him. "*After* we save a unicorn."

"A very *old* unicorn," Lucas added.

Dribble looked at him, confused. "Fortune isn't old," he said.

"Not Fortune," Princess Pulverizer explained. "There's an old unicorn who's been spotted by one of the king's knights. He's in big trouble, because the king has ordered the knights to get him a unicorn's horn."

Dribble frowned. "So now we have to find Fortune's family *and* keep the knights from capturing the old unicorn."

"Exactly," Princess Pulverizer agreed. "Good thing I know so much about unicorns. The information in this book will give us clues to places they go and how they think."

"Yes!" Dribble said. "Hopefully we know more about unicorns than those knights do. That book may come in handy."

Princess Pulverizer wanted to say "I told you so." But she didn't. Why waste time boasting when an old unicorn out there needed saving?

CHAPTER 3

"I wish we could go into the king's castle and spy on the knights. Then maybe we could find out where they spotted that old unicorn," Dribble said as he trudged

along tiredly. "*We* sure haven't seen any sign of him."

The princess and her pals had been walking quite a while, carefully remaining hidden in the bushes and trees so no one caught sight of Fortune as they searched for the old unicorn. From the top of the steepest hill they could see King Harvey's castle in the distance.

Princess Pulverizer knew the knights in that castle were probably busy planning their next move. But she also knew that wasn't going to be any help to them.

"No way we're getting in there," she replied. "The guards would stop us immediately. You can't enter a castle unless you work there, or you're really famous."

"Or if you're a member of a royal family," Lucas reminded her. "Which is how we're going to get in there."

Dribble gave him a confused look. "*We* are?"

"Well, not you and me," Lucas corrected himself. "Only her."

Princess Pulverizer gave him a look. "Her who?" she asked.

"Her *you*," Lucas replied. "The guards would surely welcome *Princess Serena of Empiria*."

"Great idea, little buddy!" Dribble cheered his pal.

"It's *not* a great idea," Princess Pulverizer insisted.

"*Why not?*" Lucas asked.

"Because being Princess Serena was awful," she replied. "Do you have any idea how boring life is when the biggest decision you make all day is whether or not to wear a tiara? That's not me. I'm not *serene*. I'm a **Pulverizer**! Which is why I changed my name."

"Do it for Fortune," Dribble pleaded. "That old unicorn is part of his family."

Fortune looked up at Princess Pulverizer and batted his long lashes.

That isn't fair. The princess wanted to help. But there had to be another way.

"No! No! No!" Princess Pulverizer repeated. "I've been working really hard learning how to swish a sword, aim an arrow, and hold a jousting lance. I don't want to go back to curtsying and remembering how to hold my pinky when I drink tea."

"Every knight has special, unique skills," Dribble told her calmly. "In your case, those skills include knowing how princesses are supposed to act."

"You're *really* Princess Pulverizer," Lucas added. "You'll just use the name Serena to get into that castle and spy on the knights."

"Your given name is just another weapon," Dribble assured her. "Like a sword, or an arrow."

"Fine," Princess Pulverizer huffed. "I'll

be Princess Serena. But just this once." She began stomping back toward Leononia.

"Whoa. Wait a minute," Dribble called out.

The princess stopped. "What now?"

"You're not getting into any castle dressed like that," the dragon said. "You need a gown."

That was true.

"You're right! Let's come up with a new plan," the princess said—a bit too happily.

"We don't need a new plan," Dribble replied. "You just need a new dress."

"Royal gowns are sewn by royal tailors," Princess Pulverizer argued. "Who work inside castles. We are *outside* the castle. So . . ."

"I thought it was such a good idea." Lucas patted Fortune on the head.

"It *is* a good idea," Dribble insisted.

"But Princess Pulverizer said . . . ,"
Lucas began.

"I heard," Dribble said. "She *will* have
royal tailors. You and I are going to create
a dress fit for a princess—or at least *this*
princess."

"You need cloth to make a gown,"
Princess Pulverizer reminded him.

Dribble looked at Lucas. "Don't you
have a red-and-white cloth in the bottom
of your knapsack?"

"How did you see my blankie . . . I
mean, blanket?!" Lucas yelped. "It was
hidden."

"You left your bag open one day,"
Dribble said. "I looked in there for some
cheese. You've been carrying that blanket
for a long time. It must be getting heavy."

"B-b-but . . ."

"You don't need a security blanket," Dribble continued. "You're not lily-livered anymore."

"Okay," Lucas said finally. He took out his blanket and handed it to Dribble. "For the old unicorn."

"This will never work," Princess Pulverizer said.

"You have a better idea?" Dribble asked.

Princess Pulverizer thought as hard as she could, but not a single idea came to her. "I've got nothing," she admitted.

"Then let's get started," Dribble said.

Princess Pulverizer frowned as Dribble draped the red-and-white flannel cloth over her shoulders and started talking about things like bell sleeves and scoop necks.

This learning-to-be-knightly thing sure wasn't turning out the way she thought it would.

CHAPTER 4

"There!" Dribble said, admiring his work. "The dress is perfect."

"Perfect?" Princess Pulverizer repeated. "Are you kidding? One sleeve's too short. The other's too long. Plus, the hem's crooked."

"Details," Dribble replied. "No one will notice."

"They better not," Princess Pulverizer huffed. She began fastening her belt around her waist.

"Stop!" Dribble exclaimed. "What are you doing?"

"Putting on my sheath," Princess Pulverizer said. "How else am I going to carry my sword?"

"You *can't* carry a sword," Dribble said.

"Why not?" Princess Pulverizer asked. "It's not like it's going to ruin the look of *this* gown."

"Nope. No sword," Dribble insisted.

"Otherwise you'd be giving yourself away."

Princess Pulverizer scowled. Boy, did she hate it when that dragon was right!

"Be careful with it," she said as she handed Dribble her sword.

"I'm aware of its truth-telling magic," Dribble assured her. "I'll keep it safe."

"Okay then," Princess Pulverizer said. "I'll be going."

"Not so fast," Dribble said.

"What *now*?" the princess demanded.

"You can't bring any arrows, either," Dribble said.

"But this is the magical arrow that points the holder toward home!" she replied.

Dribble shook his head. "Nope."

"You can wear your ruby ring," Lucas said, trying to cheer her up. "The one that lets the wearer walk in silence."

"That could come in handy," Princess Pulverizer agreed. "Especially since I'm wearing my heavy boots."

"And you have the hand mirror the good witch of Starats gave you," Lucas continued. "The one that predicts the future."

"I'll even let you borrow my magic

handkerchief," Dribble said. "The one that lets you smell things far, far away."

Wow. Dribble really valued that handkerchief. It was very generous of him to let her borrow it. Still . . .

"I don't think it's a good idea to go into that castle without a sword or arrows," Princess Pulverizer insisted. "What if I find myself in danger?"

"We'll be nearby," Lucas promised. "We can rescue you."

Rescue her! Grrr. She wasn't some damsel in distress. She was the mighty Princess Pulverizer!

Still, she couldn't just stand here arguing with Dribble and Lucas. There wasn't time. Princess Pulverizer was going into that castle, alone—with nothing but her wits to protect her.

◆ ◆ ◆ ◆ ◆

"You remember the signal?" Dribble asked
as they hid behind some trees not far from
the castle walls.

Princess Pulverizer nodded. "The trill
of a nightingale." She let out a whistle that
sounded more like the squawk of a crow.

"Close enough," Dribble said. "It won't alert anyone but us. Just another bird in the night. No one will notice anything odd. When we hear it, we will come."

"Off I go," Princess Pulverizer said, trying not to sound as nervous as she felt. "Wish me luck."

◆ ◆ ◆ ◆ ◆

"Halt in the name of King Harvey the Lion-Hearted! Who goes there?"

Thirty-two guards raised their swords and shouted in Princess Pulverizer's direction—at the exact same time.

"I am Princess Pul . . . ," she began. "I mean, I am Princess *Serena*, daughter of King Alexander of Empiria. I'm here to visit King Harvey."

"A princess? Traveling alone?" one of the guards asked suspiciously.

Well, not exactly alone. But they didn't need to know about the dragon, unicorn, and knight-in-training waiting for her nearby. So instead, Princess Pulverizer made up a story. "My guards hurried off at the sight of a large giant who lived in the woods. They took my carriage with them. They aren't nearly as brave and strong as all of you, though."

King Harvey's guards grinned. They were obviously pleased with her false praise.

"You may enter," the tallest guard said.

"Is this satisfactory, Princess Serena?" a butler asked a few minutes later, as he opened the door to a sunny yellow bedroom.

He waited for a response, but none came.

"Is there a problem, Princess Serena?"

"Huh? Oh. You're talking to me," Princess Pulverizer blurted out. "I almost forgot."

"Forgot what?" The butler sounded very confused.

"Um . . . I almost forgot how nice a room could look," Princess Pulverizer replied quickly. "I've been traveling a long time."

Phew.

"Dinner is in one hour. If you'd like to wash up, you have time." The butler gave

Princess Pulverizer a disapproving look and left, closing the door behind him.

Well, that was rude. How much of a wash could she need? All she'd done was walk into a castle. That butler should see how sweaty she got when she was doing *real* knightly stuff, like jousting in hot armor.

Although . . . she did have a bit of dirt under her fingernails. Lady Frump would never approve of dirty hands. Or messy hair, either.

Princess Pulverizer reached into her knapsack and pulled out her hand mirror to take a look at herself. But it wasn't her face that stared back from the glass.

Instead, she saw a king sitting at a long banquet table. Which was strange because dinner wasn't for an hour yet.

Then again, this was no ordinary mirror. It was a magic mirror that predicted the future.

Princess Pulverizer studied the image. There was a tiny king in a large crown, surrounded by four very large guards. That had to be King Harvey. Only a nervous king would eat surrounded by guards.

But the king *wasn't* eating. He was holding something in the air.

But what? The princess looked closer at the image.

Oh no!

In the mirror, King Harvey was holding up a long pointed horn. *An alicorn!*

Princess Pulverizer had arrived too late. While Dribble and Lucas were busy making this stupid dress, the knights had been busy capturing the old unicorn and

presenting the king with his horn.

Princess Pulverizer tried to think calmly.
After all, real knights never panicked. At
least she didn't think they did.

Maybe this wasn't as bad as it looked.
There could still be time to help the old
unicorn. After all, the mirror didn't give
any clue as to how far in the future this

was taking place. It might not be tonight's dinner. It could be tomorrow. Or next week. Or even next month.

Princess Pulverizer didn't know if there was a way to change the future and the image in the mirror from coming

She just knew she was going to try.

CHAPTER 5

As she took her seat at the king's table, Princess Pulverizer found herself growing more and more concerned. And not just about the old unicorn.

She was also worried about all the silverware that had been laid out in front of her.

Was the big spoon for soup or dessert?

What was that teeny tiny fork for?

Which water glass should she use?

Princess Pulverizer wished she'd paid more attention to Lady Frump's lecture on fancy dining. Because if she couldn't figure this stuff out, no one would be fooled into thinking Princess Pulverizer was an actual princess.

Even though she was.

If King Harvey thought for one minute that there was a spy in his midst, there was no telling what he might do.

Just then, the doors of the banquet hall opened. King Harvey walked into the room, surrounded by four large guards.

"Hello, friends," King Harvey said.

Princess Pulverizer choked back a laugh. She'd expected King Harvey the Lion-Hearted to have a big strong voice. Instead, he squeaked when he spoke.

Oops! Princess Pulverizer had dropped her napkin under the table. She bent down to pick it up and—

Thud! She bumped her head on the hard wooden table.

"Yikes! What was that?" King Harvey the Lion-Hearted grabbed one of his guards and held on tight for dear life.

"Sorry," Princess Pulverizer apologized. "I dropped my napkin."

"N-no problem." King Harvey loosened his grip on the guard and turned his attention to the butler. "Have the kitchen staff serve the first course," he commanded.

The butler bowed and headed off. Not a moment later, there was a loud crash, like the sound of a pot falling from the shelf.

"AAAAAHHHHH!" King Harvey leaped out of his seat so fast he reminded Princess Pulverizer of the jack-in-the-box toy she'd played with as a little girl.

Oddly, no one else seemed to notice the king's strange behavior. They must have seen him act that way before.

"I'm sorry," the butler apologized as he came running back into the banquet hall. "There was a slight collision in the kitchen. The first course will be here any minute."

Princess Pulverizer was starving. Luckily, a fresh-baked roll had been placed on the small plate in front of her. The princess bit off a huge hunk and turned to the woman seated to her right.

"Do you know what's for dinner?" she asked her.

The woman made a face. But she didn't answer.

Hmmm . . . the princess thought. *Maybe she can't hear so well.*

"DO YOU KNOW WHAT'S FOR DINNER?" the princess shouted at her. A piece of bread flew out of her mouth and onto the woman's face.

Oops. The princess had forgotten what Lady Frump had told her so many times: Princesses do not speak with their mouths full.

And if she wasn't mistaken, no one began eating until the king did, either. She was doing *everything* wrong.

"The royal soup, sir!" the butler announced as he returned to the banquet hall.

"Very good," King Harvey replied. "You may serve."

Princess Pulverizer watched as royal waiters ladled creamy navy-bean soup into each soup bowl. Her stomach gurgled in excitement, which wasn't very princess-y. But she couldn't help it.

"Would you like me to get the royal taster, sir?" the butler asked.

"No need," King Harvey replied. "One of my knights has given me something very special to prevent poisoning."

Princess Pulverizer frowned. The

picture she had seen in the mirror was almost complete. There was little King Harvey, with his very large crown, seated at the head of the table, surrounded by four guards.

The only thing missing was—

"*A unicorn horn,*" the king said as he held up a long, pointed horn. "This will protect me from poison."

Everyone began talking at once.

"A unicorn horn!"

"How marvelous."

"All hail King Harvey's royal knights."

Princess Pulverizer didn't say a word. She was too busy staring at the horn. There was something odd about it. Something she hadn't noticed in the magic mirror. "That horn is not from a unicorn!" she exclaimed suddenly.

Everyone turned to look at her.

"I beg your pardon?" King Harvey demanded.

"That horn is not from a unicorn," Princes Pulverizer repeated. "It's too smooth. Unicorns have spiraled horns. That one might be from a rhinoceros. Or a walrus."

Once again, everyone began talking.

"How does she know that?"

"Did a knight lie to the king?"

"She ate her roll before the meal began. Can we trust her?"

"I can prove that's not a real alicorn," Princess Pulverizer said.

"A real what?" one gentleman seated near her asked.

"Alicorn," Princess Pulverizer repeated. "That's what you call a unicorn's horn."

"She's a know-it-all," one woman complained.

"What happened to princesses being seen and not heard?" asked another.

Princess Pulverizer had *never* been seen and not heard. She wasn't about to start now. "There is a way to test if an alicorn is real," she continued. "Place it in cold water. If that horn really came from a unicorn, the water will bubble as if it were boiling, but it will still be cold."

"Bring me a bowl of cold water!" the king demanded.

The king's butler scurried into the kitchen. He returned a moment later with a bowl of cold water.

"My knights would never lie to me," the king insisted. "I will prove it." He dropped the alicorn in the bowl and waited.

But the water did not bubble.

"I told you so," Princess Pulverizer said proudly.

A murmur went through the room.

"How rude."

"Did she just tell the king 'I told you so'?"

"He's going to be angry."

"I will not have this!" King Harvey squawked furiously.

Uh-oh.

"I will not have my knights lying to me!" the king continued.

Phew. King Harvey wasn't angry with Princess Pulverizer after all. He was mad at his knights. The princess was very relieved.

But not for long.

Because just then King Harvey declared, "I hereby decree that no one in this kingdom shall eat or drink anything until I have a real alicorn. So I suggest the knights find a unicorn and bring me his horn on a silver platter . . . *quickly*."

CHapter 6

I should have let him believe it was an alicorn, Princess Pulverizer thought regretfully. *He wouldn't have known the difference. And he would have left the old unicorn*

alone. Why do I always have to show off?

Still, there was no point thinking about should-haves or would-haves. What the princess needed to do now was find a way to save the old unicorn.

That was why she was standing quietly behind a curtain in the knights' drawing room, eavesdropping as they plotted. The princess had snuck into the room right behind the knights. It had been so easy. The knights had been huddled together and so focused on coming up with a plan, they never noticed her.

The princess rubbed her ruby ring gratefully. It had done its job, allowing her to enter the room in complete silence.

"Do you think the old unicorn is still where you spotted him, Gordon?" the princess heard a knight ask.

"He's probably moved on, Humphrey," Gordon admitted. "To keep from being caught. Although he didn't look like he could go *too* far. He was really old. His beard nearly hit the ground. His fur had turned green and yellow. And he was just sitting there under those long, drooping branches, barely moving."

"Do unicorns go green when they're old?" a third knight wondered. "People go gray."

"Unicorns are different from people, Filippo," Gordon reminded him.

That is true. But Princess Pulverizer figured most likely the old unicorn's fur was green and yellow because he was hiding among trees that had green leaves and yellow flowers.

Clearly Gordon had not read the book

Unicorns from A to Z.

"Are you sure it was an actual unicorn?" Filippo asked Gordon. "Maybe it was a horse."

"Horses don't have beards or horns," Gordon told him. "I should've grabbed him when I had the chance. But I felt sorry for him. He was so feeble. It didn't seem like a fair fight. I figured the king would surely be fooled by that old walrus horn I got at a market."

Princess Pulverizer was impressed. What a knightly thing of Gordon to do! He would have gotten away with it too—if she hadn't opened her big mouth.

"Well, we have to catch him now," Humphrey insisted. "We have a direct order—and very empty stomachs—to fill."

"I don't think King Harvey will be

satisfied with just one horn," Gordon said. "What's going to happen when he breaks it?"

"He *is* always breaking things," Filippo agreed. "Remember when he was about to toast the Queen of Hammerhousen, and a bird tweeted outside the window? He got so scared he dropped the glass."

"When he breaks the horn, we'll go hungry again," Gordon said. "We should get him some spares."

"If there's an old unicorn around, younger ones can't be too far away," Humphrey suggested. "We can track them down and get *all* their horns."

"Let's head out first thing in the morning," Filippo added. "We are excellent animal trackers. I bet we'll be eating again by lunch!"

This was even worse than Princess Pulverizer had feared. She had to warn the unicorns! Without thinking, she slipped from behind the curtain and raced to the door.

The knights stared at her with surprise.

"Where'd *she* come from?" Gordon asked as she whizzed by him.

"Do you think she heard us?" Filippo wondered.

"It doesn't matter," Humphrey told them. "She's just

some princess. What can she do to stop us?"

Humphrey was a fool. She wasn't just some princess. She was *Princess Pulverizer*. And she *was* going to stop the knights from harming the unicorns. They would just have to wait and see.

CHAPTER 7

"Halt! Who goes there?"

Princess Pulverizer stopped at the castle gates and looked up at the thirty two guards.

"Princess Serena. I'm leaving." Princess Pulverizer was surprised how much easier the name Serena came to her lips now.

"Leaving?" the guard asked. "Do you have permission? King Harvey doesn't like us opening the gates for just anyone."

"Why would I need permission to *leave*?" Princess Pulverizer asked him. "What threat is someone who isn't going to be here anymore?"

The guards looked at one another. The princess got the feeling no one had presented them with that idea before.

"Fine." The tallest guard pushed open the gate and looked onto the street. "Where's your carriage?"

Uh-oh.

"I'm . . . um . . . walking," Princess Pulverizer said. "My guards and carriage have still not returned."

"Princesses don't walk alone at night," the guard insisted.

"This princess does," Princess Pulverizer replied defiantly. "We're not all alike, you know."

With that, the princess shot off like a jackrabbit, only stopping when she found a quiet alleyway, far from the castle walls.

Princess Pulverizer took a moment to catch her breath, and finally let out a loud nightingale whistle.

Then she waited for Dribble and Lucas to come running to her side.

And waited.

And waited some more.

Clink. Clank.

The princess heard the sound of armor coming in her direction.

Thud. Thud. Thud.

The ground began to shake.

Gulp. Had the king's knights figured out Princess Pulverizer was a real threat to their plans? Were they coming to stop her? The princess's heart pounded so hard she thought it might leap out of her chest. Until . . .

"Sorry it took us a while," Dribble apologized as he, Lucas, and Fortune came racing toward her.

What a relief! The ground had been shaking under Dribble's weight. And the clinking armor she'd heard belonged to Lucas.

"We had trouble with Fortune," Lucas explained. "He wanted a bite of someone's roses, so he stuck his head between the fence posts."

"Then he couldn't get his head *out*," Dribble added.

"You're always getting into trouble, aren't you?" Princess Pulverizer said. She petted the unicorn's head. *Yuck!* "Why is he greasy?"

"Butter," Dribble said. "We used it to make him slippery so we could slide him loose."

Princess Pulverizer wiped her hands on her red-and-white dress. No need for a napkin *here*.

"It's worse than we thought," she said, getting straight down to business. "The knights don't just want to capture the old unicorn. They want to capture *all* the unicorns."

"We have to stop them!" Lucas declared.

"Obviously," Dribble agreed. "But how?"

Lucas and Dribble both stared at the princess, hoping she had a plan.

"I have no clue," she said. "But I do know the old unicorn is hiding among some willow trees."

"Are you sure?" Lucas asked her.

"Pretty sure," she admitted. "According to a knight named Gordon, the tree where the unicorn was hiding had drooping branches. And he said the old unicorn had a yellow and green coat. Willows have drooping branches with green leaves and yellow flowers. I think the unicorn changed colors to blend in."

"It makes sense," Dribble said. "Willows give a lot of shade. An old unicorn would want to be somewhere cool and comfortable."

"I'm sure the other unicorns know that, too," Princess Pulverizer agreed. "Which means they'll look for him among some willows. And if Gordon goes back to where he first saw the old unicorn, and the other unicorns should happen to arrive when the knights do—"

The princess stopped midsentence. She didn't want to think about what might happen.

"We have to get to him quickly," Princess Pulverizer said instead. "It's getting late, and the knights are going to start looking for the unicorns at dawn."

"How would someone go about tracking a unicorn anyway?" Lucas wondered.

"Start looking for clues, I suppose," Dribble replied. "Like fur that's been shed, or hoofprints."

"That's it!" Princess Pulverizer exclaimed suddenly.

"What's it?" Lucas asked her.

"Hoofprints," she replied. "If the knights are tracking unicorns, we're going to set them off track. *Really* off track!"

◆ ◆ ◆ ◆ ◆

"Do you think the knights will be fooled by these?" Lucas held up the clay shoe he'd just crafted. The sole was shaped exactly like a unicorn's hoof.

"I hope so." Princess Pulverizer carefully slipped her foot into one of the clay shoes she'd sculpted and smiled up at Dribble. "You're right. This mud dries *really* fast."

The princess began to walk around. Everywhere she stepped she left a unicorn hoofprint. It worked!

"Everybody have clay shoes on?" Princess Pulverizer asked Dribble, Lucas, and Fortune.

Her friends all nodded. Well, Lucas and Dribble did anyway. Fortune was busy dining on a daffodil. Then again, *he* didn't need clay shoes to leave unicorn tracks.

"All we have to do is run around leaving fake tracks for the knights to follow," Princess Pulverizer instructed. "Just be sure to stay away from any place real unicorns might be actually hiding—like flower gardens."

"Speaking of which, I'd better keep an eye on Fortune," Dribble said. "I don't want him running off to feast on someone's forget-me-nots."

"Perfect," Princess Pulverizer agreed. "We'll meet behind the cottages near the castle just before dawn."

The princess reached into her knapsack and yanked out a candle that she had found in Sir Surly's cottage, back when she and her friends had been in Yabko-kokomo.

She pulled out her sword. It felt good to have her weapons back—even if this time the sword of truth was only being used to cut a candle into three parts, making sure to leave a small piece of wick at the top of each one.

"These will light your way," she said as she handed the bits of candle to her friends. "Now let's make tracks!"

chapter 8

Princess Pulverizer yawned and rubbed her eyes. It had been a long night. She'd walked for miles leaving fake hoofprints in places unicorns would never actually go.

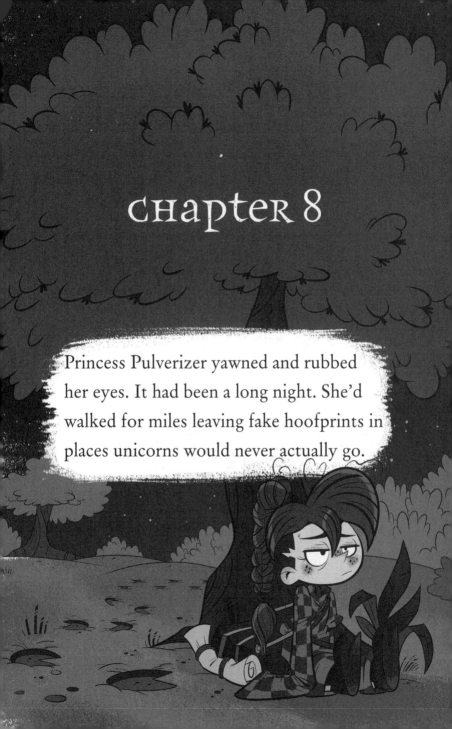

It would be nice to close her eyes for a few minutes. Then she—ZZZZ . . .

"WHAT ARE YOU DOING?"

Dribble's thunderous shout bolted Princess Pulverizer upright from her slumber.

"How can you sleep?" the dragon demanded. "The sun is almost up. Those knights are about to go on their hunt."

The princess blinked twice and looked up at Dribble, Fortune, and Lucas.

"I wasn't sleeping," she insisted.

"Are you kidding?" Dribble asked. "You were snoring louder than a yeti."

Princess Pulverizer was about to reply when she heard the familiar sound of a trumpet blaring. She knew what that meant.

"Come on!" The princess scrambled to

her feet. "The hunt has started!"

"I can't believe they're falling for those fake hoofprints I left," Princess Pulverizer said. The sun was bright now, and she and her pals were hiding behind a clump of trees, watching the knights on their hunt.

"Everyone knows unicorns don't use public bathrooms."

"They don't use *private* bathrooms, either." Lucas giggled.

"No unicorns in here," Gordon shouted to the others as he walked out of the outhouse. "But it does *smell* beastly."

"I found more tracks!" Filippo called.

Gordon and Humphrey went running.

Princess Pulverizer and her pals snuck quietly behind some fences and a building, following them.

"These lead to Mr. Wasserbagel's bakery," Filippo said. "I'm hungry. Maybe we can get a cookie while we look?"

"King Harvey said no eating until we bring him that horn," Gordon replied.

"The door's locked anyway," Humphrey added.

Gordon looked around the side of the shop. "Here are some other tracks," he said. "They seem to be pointing toward Farmer Silosorter's fields, leading toward the corn maze he created for the harvest festival."

"Wow! Look at the size of *those* hoofprints," Humphrey added. "That unicorn must be massive. I bet he's the leader!"

Dribble stood tall and puffed his green chest proudly.

"Don't get any ideas," Princess Pulverizer whispered. "Your feet—and therefore your shoes—are just bigger than ours. That doesn't make you the leader."

The princess and her pals continued sneaking behind the knights as they followed more hoofprints.

"I think they're hiding in here!" Gordon exclaimed, stopping at the edge of a large corn field.

"You guys left hoofprints in the corn maze?" Princess Pulverizer asked Dribble.

"Now it's a *uni*-corn maze." Dribble laughed. "You're not the only one who can tell a good joke."

"These tracks lead right," Filippo said.

"But those lead left," Humphrey added.

"And some go straight ahead," Gordon noted.

CLANG.

CLINK.

CLONK.

"Watch where you're going!" Princess Pulverizer heard Gordon yell as his armored body banged into one of his friends.

"You crashed into *me*!" Humphrey argued.

"Those knights will be lost in that maze for hours," Dribble boasted.

"Giving us enough time to find the real unicorns," Princess Pulverizer said. "At least I hope so."

CHAPTER 9

Aaachoooo! Dribble sneezed loudly.

"Quiet," Princess Pulverizer warned. "You don't want to scare the old unicorn if he's hiding behind those trees."

"I can't help it. I'm allergic to willows," Dribble replied.

"The old unicorn isn't here," Lucas said as he peered under the branches of a big willow tree. "This is the third grove we've searched. I doubt we're ever going to find him, or anyone else from Fortune's blessing."

"Maybe we're going about this all wrong," Dribble said. "We assumed Gordon spotted the old unicorn near Leononia. But knights travel everywhere. What if he saw him somewhere else? Like the meadow near Beeten Wheeten where Fortune came from."

"The old unicorn might have been too weak to search for Fortune with the others. He could have stayed behind," Lucas agreed.

"Exactly," Dribble continued. "If the old unicorn poked his head out of hiding for even a moment, and Gordon surprised him, they might have seen one another."

"Poor old unicorn," Lucas said. "If you're right, he's been alone a long time. It's been days since the others went out looking for Fortune."

"They may have returned to check on the old guy," Dribble suggested. "In fact, the whole blessing could be there right now. We should go back to the meadow where Fortune came from and see."

"Good idea," Lucas agreed.

Princess Pulverizer shook her head. "It's *not* a good idea," she insisted.

"Why not?" Dribble asked.

"Because we don't know how to *get* back to Fortune's home," she replied.

"It's just outside of Beeten Wheeten," Lucas reminded her. "All we have to do is head back that way."

"Except we've taken a lot of roads since we left Beeten Wheeten," Princess Pulverizer argued. "I have no idea how to get back there. Do you?"

"We're all turned around. We'd never find our way back there," Lucas said with a heavy sigh. "This is beginning to seem so pointless."

"*Point*less!" Princess Pulverizer exclaimed excitedly. "That's it!"

Dribble and Lucas stared at her, confused.

"Fortune can lead us back," the princess explained. "All he needs is the magic arrow—the one that *points* the holder toward his home."

Quickly, the princess began braiding the arrow with orange and yellow feathers into Fortune's tail.

"Why don't you just stick it in his mouth?" Lucas asked.

"This guy?" Princess Pulverizer asked. "He'll just eat it. Or, at the very least, break it with his teeth."

The princess finished off the braid, and stood back to admire her work. Almost immediately, the unicorn's tail began to twitch and turn. Finally, it pointed to the left.

Fortune jumped up in surprise. And then, he began to walk—*backward*—in the direction his tail pointed.

"It's working!" Lucas exclaimed
excitedly.

"Sure is," Dribble agreed.

"I don't know why you guys ever doubt
me," Princess Pulverizer said smugly. "*I*
certainly never do."

"I recognize those shimmery flowers," Princess Pulverizer said a long while later as she looked around the flowery meadow where the arrow had led them. "This is definitely Fortune's home." She unbraided the arrow from Fortune's tail and smiled.

"With all these flowers, and that brook, it's the perfect spot for unicorns," Lucas added. "It's got everything."

"Except *unicorns*," Dribble pointed out sadly. "I don't see a single one. I guess I was wrong."

Suddenly, Fortune reared up on his hind legs and began twirling in circles. Then he let out a series of cooing noises.

"What's with him?" Dribble wondered.

"He's dancing," Princess Pulverizer said. "And singing, I think."

A chorus of coos echoed back from the

bushes and trees. It sounded like a whole flock of turtledoves were hiding there.

Only it wasn't a flock of birds.

It was a blessing of *unicorns*. And now they were all running toward the center of the meadow.

They leaped from the lavender.

Raced from the rosebushes.

And trotted out from among the trumpet vines.

"Camouflage is a very handy trick," Lucas said. "I didn't see a single unicorn at first."

"They were probably afraid of us," Dribble replied. "But once Fortune let them know it was safe, they came out."

Fortune was now joyously touching horns with the other unicorns. Princess Pulverizer was happy to see Fortune dancing with his family.

But she was *un*happy about what she *didn't* see.

The meadow was filled with big unicorns, small unicorns, fat unicorns, and thin unicorns. But there wasn't a single *old* unicorn.

Fortune wandered over to a willow tree and nudged his horn in between the green leaves and yellow flowers.

Coo. Fortune let out a gentle, quiet call.

Coo. The answer came back just as quietly.

Princess Pulverizer peered over Fortune's back. Sitting there among the flowering branches was an old green-and-yellow-furred unicorn. The coloring had helped him blend in with the flowers and leaves, but the princess now saw his blue eyes and pointed horn.

The old unicorn looked at Fortune, but did not leap to his feet to greet him as the others had. Princess Pulverizer doubted he could. He looked so tired and frail.

"I wonder how long he's been sitting there," Dribble said.

Princess Pulverizer figured it was possible he'd been there all along—even when they'd first brought Fortune here to look for his blessing. He blended in so well with the willows, it was impossible to see him.

The other unicorns gathered around the old unicorn. They moved in, blocking him from sight.

Protecting him.

But they couldn't keep the old unicorn safe here forever. Sooner or later, the knights would find their way out of that corn maze and come back here—to where Gordon must have first spotted the old unicorn.

And while Princess Pulverizer, Lucas, and Dribble had the power of three, so did Gordon, Filippo, and Humphrey. To make matters worse, *they* were already knights, with more weapons than the princess and her pals had. That was not a battle Princess Pulverizer could win.

But the princess was not giving up. She *would* save all the unicorns. There had to be a way. Unfortunately, she didn't know what it was.

Yet.

CHAPTER 10

*How can we get the old unicorn
moving?*

Princess Pulverizer
was struggling to
come up with an
idea. But so far
not a single plan
had come into
her head.

"Do you think our mace would heal him?" Lucas wondered.

Princess Pulverizer knew Lucas was talking about the huge mace they'd received as a gift from the king of Yabko-kokomo. It had the power to heal the wounds of anyone on the side of all that was good and right.

"It's worth a try." Dribble lifted the heavy golden mace and waved it over the unicorn.

Then they waited.

And waited.

And waited.

"Nothing's happening," Lucas said finally.

"Maybe this unicorn isn't a good guy?" Dribble wondered.

Princess Pulverizer shook her head. "I

don't think being a good guy has anything to do with it," she said. "The problem is, he isn't injured. He's just old. Even a magic mace can't change that."

"Too bad we can't just put him in a giant carriage and give him a ride," Lucas said.

"Lucas, you're a genius!" Princess Pulverizer exclaimed.

"Thanks," Lucas replied proudly. Then he paused and thought for a moment. "Wait. *Why* am I a genius?"

Princess Pulverizer didn't answer. She was too busy rolling a thick fallen log toward the middle of the meadow.

"What are you doing?" Dribble asked her, confused.

"Building a carriage," Princess Pulverizer responded. "Well, probably more like a sled. For the old unicorn."

"A sled?" Dribble repeated, still confused.

"Yup!" Princess Pulverizer rolled another old log over.

"Don't you think he's a bit too old to go sledding?" Dribble asked. "And I don't see any snow on the ground."

"It's more like he's going to go *sliding*," Princess Pulverizer explained. "We'll get the old unicorn on the sled. Then the rest of his blessing can pull him someplace safe."

"How do you propose we build a sled?" Dribble asked her.

"We'll use strands of ivy to tie logs and branches together," the princess replied.

"Are unicorns powerful enough to pull a sled?" Lucas wondered.

"According to *Unicorns from A to Z*,

they are strong
enough to defeat
elephants," the
princess answered.
"So I imagine so."

Dribble went
over to a large tree.
He leaped up and
grabbed on to a
thick branch. Then
he hung there in midair, his feet dangling.

"What are you doing?" Princess
Pulverizer asked him. "We don't have time
for you to practice your pull-ups."

"I'm not exercising," Dribble said.
"I'm—"

Crack! The branch broke off from
the tree and Dribble landed hard on the
ground.

"—helping you," Dribble continued, dragging the thick branch over to where the princess was building her sled. "How much more wood will we need?"

"Push harder!" Princess Pulverizer ordered. "We've almost got him on the sled."

"I'm trying," Dribble replied as he pushed hard on the unicorn's back end. "Unicorns are heavy."

The old unicorn let out a small moan.

"Careful. You don't want to break him," Lucas said.

"I don't think you can break a unicorn," Dribble replied. "Besides, he's on the sled now."

"Great!" Princess Pulverizer exclaimed.

"I'll hand the reins to the other unicorns, and they can get pulling."

"How are we going to get them to understand that we *want* them to pull?" Dribble asked her.

Princess Pulverizer frowned. "No idea."

"Maybe we could *show* them how to do it," Lucas suggested.

"That's a good idea," Princess Pulverizer agreed. "I'll pretend to be the old unicorn, and you two can pull me."

The princess sat down and held tight to the ends of two vines. "Now, you guys take the other ends and pull."

Dribble and Lucas each pulled hard on the vines. The princess slid along on her bottom.

The unicorns didn't move.

"They don't get it," Princess Pulverizer

said. "Maybe you guys should prance—
you know, like unicorns do."

"Are you *kidding*?" Dribble bellowed.

"Come on, Dribble," Lucas pleaded.
"For Fortune and his friends."

"Fine," Dribble grumbled. He and Lucas
began to prance while Princess Pulverizer
scooted around on her rear end.

Fortune and his friends looked at them strangely. And then . . .

The unicorns began to prance!

"They understand!" Princess Pulverizer exclaimed. "This is going to work!"

As she fastened one end of the reins securely around Fortune's middle, Princess Pulverizer whispered into his ear. "Stay safe."

Fortune nuzzled against her. Then he turned to the others in his blessing and let out a powerful shout. In a flash, the team of unicorns was off, pulling the sled that carried the eldest of them deep into the woods.

"Will they be okay?" Lucas wondered.

"Unicorns have been hiding for a very

long time," Dribble assured him.

"I'm going to miss Fortune," Princess Pulverizer admitted. She blinked hard.

"Are you crying?" Dribble asked.

Princess Pulverizer wiped her eyes. "No," she lied. "It's these flowers. You're not the only one who can have allergies."

Dribble smiled. "We did a very good deed," he assured her.

"Only we didn't get a token of gratitude," Lucas told Princess Pulverizer. "This good deed won't help you on your Quest of Kindness. I'm so sorry."

"It's okay," Princess Pulverizer said with a shrug. "Fortune's blessing got away safely. That's what's important. Let's go into the city and buy some fresh supplies so we can move on."

As Princess Pulverizer headed back

toward Leononia, Dribble and Lucas stood there, staring at her.

"Boy, she's really changed," Lucas said.

"Definitely," Dribble agreed.

"What are you waiting for?" Princess Pulverizer demanded. "I swear, from now on, I'm going to call you two Slow and Poke!"

Dribble rolled his eyes. "Or, maybe not," he grumbled as he followed the princess down the road.

CHAPTER 11

"WHAT DO YOU MEAN YOU COULDN'T FIND THAT UNICORN?"

King Harvey's squeaky voice hurt Princess Pulverizer's ears as she stood near the castle gates, hidden behind a group of hungry people who had gathered to cheer the knights' return.

The king, too, had been waiting at the gate, eager to greet his knights when they returned with a unicorn horn. But they'd returned empty-handed.

"I'm sorry, sir," Humphrey apologized. "We tried, but the unicorns have disappeared."

"I want a unicorn horn!" King Harvey began jumping up and down like a toddler having a tantrum. "I want one! I want one!"

Princess Pulverizer laughed so hard she snorted. *Loudly*.

The people around her moved away quickly. No one wanted to be near anyone who laughed at King Harvey.

"I know you!" King Harvey shouted as he spotted the princess. "You're that know-it-all. And . . . YIKES! Is that a dragon?"

"Yes," Princess Pulverizer answered.

"But you don't have to worry about Dribble. He's . . ."

"You're a spy!" King Harvey declared. "Not only have you returned accompanied by a knight ready for battle, you've brought a dragon to burn down my castle."

"I'm only a knight-*in-training*," Lucas said. "Or I used to be, before some mean kids laughed me out of Knight School."

"And I don't burn down castles," Dribble insisted. "I make grilled cheese."

"Bring the enemies to my quarters!" the king ordered. "I'll question them myself."

"When we met, you seemed to know a lot about unicorns," King Harvey reminded Princess Pulverizer a few minutes later. "You must know where they are hiding."

"I have no idea," Princess Pulverizer replied.

The sword of truth lay still by the princess's side. She really didn't know where Fortune and his blessing had gone.

"Tell me," King Harvey insisted, "or you will all spend the rest of your days in my dungeon."

"Oh dear." Lucas looked as though he might cry.

Princess Pulverizer didn't blame him. That sounded pretty dismal. She struggled to think of some way to make the king happy. But before she could come up with anything, there was a knock at the door.

"Who goes there?" a guard demanded.

"Professor Coggin-Noggin of the Royal

University. I must speak to the king *about unicorns*."

Princess Pulverizer and her friends exchanged nervous glances.

"Enter!" King Harvey squealed excitedly.

"Your majesty, you can end your search for the unicorns," Professor Coggin-Noggin declared as he hurried into the room.

"Why would I do that?" King Harvey demanded.

"Because unicorns do *not* exist," Professor Coggin-Noggin replied. "They're only found in fairy tales. I've done my research. And I am the smartest person in Leononia."

"I beg your pardon?" King Harvey squeaked angrily.

"Other than you, of course," Professor Coggin-Noggin corrected himself.

Princess Pulverizer rolled her eyes. If Professor Coggin-Noggin was the smartest man in Leononia, this place was in trouble. Because unicorns *did* exist.

But she didn't say that. She'd learned her lesson. The unicorns were safer if folks thought they were make-believe.

"Now that the unicorn question has been settled, we'll be on our way," she said instead.

"You aren't going anywhere!" King Harvey told her. "You're still in trouble. You came to my banquet under false pretenses. You're no princess."

"She is," Lucas insisted. "She's just a different *kind* of princess. She's more like a knight."

"She's more like an *enemy*," King Harvey corrected him. "I don't trust any of you. So I'm going to keep you where you can't hurt me—in the dungeon!"

A bead of nervous perspiration dripped from the princess's upper lip.

Oh no! She'd broken one of her father's knights' most important rules: Never let your enemies see you sweat.

The princess started to wipe her face with her hand, but Dribble kindly handed her his handkerchief. The princess used the cloth to wipe away the beads of sweat that had formed just below her nose.

Suddenly she smelled flowers—Queen Anne's lace, lavender, yarrow, and foxglove.

How strange. There wasn't a single blossom in the room.

But there were flowers outside the castle walls. By holding Dribble's magic handkerchief near her nose, Princess Pulverizer was able to smell things that were far away.

If only King Harvey weren't so afraid all

the time. If only he could just relax. Take a little time to smell the . . .

Flowers!

"That's it!" Princess Pulverizer shouted out excitedly. "You don't need a unicorn horn. You can protect yourself just by visiting flower shops."

"That's ridiculous," the king scoffed.

"It's not," Princess Pulverizer insisted. "Some people say that flowers have mystical powers—like the ability to protect against evil. I learned about it in Lady Frump's flower-arranging class."

At the time, Princess Pulverizer had thought learning about flowers was really silly. But that knowledge actually might come in handy now.

"There's columbine, flower of loyalty," she continued. "Violets safeguard against evil. Queen Anne's lace is a symbol of a safe space, and yarrow is the symbol of good health."

"Why have *I* never heard of the power of flowers?" King Harvey wondered.

"Because you never went to the Royal School of Ladylike Manners, I suppose," Princess Pulverizer replied.

"What do you think of this, Coggin-Noggin?" King Harvey asked.

"A cup of lavender tea did soothe my stomach after I ate brussels sprouts at supper last Sunday," the professor said. "I hate brussels sprouts. They smell like feet."

"Feet that haven't been washed," Princess Pulverizer added.

Ahem. King Harvey cleared his throat. "Can we get back to *my* problem?"

"I suppose there is some proof that flowers can protect humans from ailments," Professor Coggin Noggin told him. "Perhaps even illnesses brought on by poisoning."

"Fine," the king said. "I shall send my knights out to pick all the wildflowers in the countryside."

"NO!" Princess Pulverizer shouted.

"Why not?" the king demanded.

The princess did not want the knights going anywhere near wildflowers. They might stumble upon the unicorns eating.

"Those wildflowers are helping keep your subjects in the countryside safe," the princess said, thinking quickly. "As a good king, you want that, right?"

"Um . . . of course," King Harvey replied. But he sounded less worried about his subjects than himself.

"Why not purchase flowers from shop owners?" Lucas added. "It would help their businesses. If *you* buy flowers, everyone will."

"I *am* a trendsetter," the king agreed. "Guard, send my knights out to all the florists. Tell them to come back with the biggest bouquets ever seen."

As the guard left to deliver the message, King Harvey shot Princess Pulverizer and her pals a stern look. "This had best not be a trick," he warned. "Or you will be sorry."

CHAPTER 12

This better work. Princess Pulverizer's mind raced nervously as she watched King Harvey take a bite of his three-bean salad. If the king thought for one moment he was being poisoned, she and her friends were in big trouble.

AAACHOOO! Dribble let out a massive sneeze.

"Silence!" King Harvey shouted at him.

"I can't help it," Dribble replied. "There

are so many flowers here." *AAACHOOO!*

Lucas patted his friend on the back and bit his lip nervously. Being brave didn't come naturally to Lucas.

Princess Pulverizer looked around the banquet hall. No wonder Dribble was sneezing. There were an awful lot of flowers.

Gladioli for faithfulness.

Heather and foxgloves for protection.

And giant sunflowers for health and vitality. The king had taken the princess's advice very seriously.

This better work.

"Your chamomile-flower tea, sir."

The butler poured steaming yellow tea into the king's cup.

"This better work," King Harvey told the princess.

Exactly what I was thinking, she agreed silently.

The king took a sip of the tea. Immediately his face turned beet red and his eyes began to bulge.

Princess Pulverizer's heart started pounding. Had King Harvey really been poisoned?

"Too hot!" King Harvey shouted.

Phew. Is that all?

"Tea is best served hot, your majesty," Professor Coggin-Noggin reminded him. "Perhaps you should blow on it."

"Very wise, Professor." The king blew on the tea and took a big sip.

"Do you feel ill, your majesty?" Professor Coggin-Noggin asked.

The king touched his stomach.

He wiggled around in his seat.

And opened his mouth as if to burp.

But not a single sound came out of him.

"I feel quite well!" the king announced happily. "The flowers protected me from being poisoned."

More likely the chamomile tea had settled the gas in his stomach. But Princess Pulverizer was willing to let the king believe anything he wanted, as long as she could leave Leononia. She was a know-it-all no more.

"Right," Princess Pulverizer told the king. "Now that you're safe, we'll be going. Nice to have met you."

The princess hurried toward the door,

‹131›

with Lucas and Dribble following close behind.

"Guards! Stop them!" King Harvey ordered.

Two guards leaped in front of Princess Pulverizer and her friends.

The princess gulped. *What now?*

"We're not your enemies, your majesty," Princess Pulverizer insisted. "We *helped* you."

"I know," King Harvey replied. "I wish to thank you properly."

AAACHOOO! Dribble sneezed again. "I really gotta go," he said.

"This will only take a moment," the king said. He opened a drawer and pulled out a velvet box. "This pendant belonged to my father. He wore it in the battle against Panthera. The lion charm has a magic power—it brings the wearer great bravery."

"So why do you keep it in a box instead of wearing it?" Princess Pulverizer asked.

Oops. Maybe that had been a bit rude.

But the king didn't seem to notice. "I guess I was afraid I'd lose it," he admitted.

Princess Pulverizer choked back a laugh. What *wasn't* this king afraid of?

"Anyway, I'd like you to have it now," the king continued.

Princess Pulverizer didn't need a charm to make her brave. She was already pretty fearless. But she did know someone who could use a little bravery.

"Lucas should have that pendant," Princess Pulverizer told King Harvey. "He has done some brave things. With that charm I am sure he will do many more."

"Me?" Lucas asked.

"Sure. You gave up your blanket to help our friends," Princess Pulverizer said, being very careful not to mention that those friends were *unicorns*. "That took a lot of courage."

"I will miss my blankie," Lucas admitted.

King Harvey fastened the chain around Lucas's neck.

"Thank you, sir," Lucas said with a bow.

"Thank *you*," King Harvey replied.

"We'll be going now," Princess Pulverizer told the king. She was anxious to get on to her next adventure.

"I hope to see you again," the king replied.

With that the princess and her pals

headed out of the castle. But just as they walked through the gates, a huge bee flew out from a newly planted garden of white carnations—the flower of strength and power.

Lucas stopped in his tracks. He stared nervously at the bee. Then he rubbed his finger over the lion charm on its chain around his neck.

The bee came right up to Lucas's nose.

But Lucas didn't scream. Or shout. Or leap about.

He simply swatted that bee away!

Princess Pulverizer was impressed. Maybe the lion charm really *did* work.

A while later, Princess Pulverizer and her friends found themselves strolling along on a dirt road leading away from Leononia. The princess was all smiles, thinking about the new adventures that awaited her.

Suddenly, Lucas took off like a bolt of lightning.

"What's the hurry?" the princess asked as he zoomed past her.

"There could be someone in trouble," Lucas called back, rubbing his lion charm. "We need to get to them quickly. This is no time for a stroll."

Lucas? *Looking* for trouble? Wow. That charm sure was powerful.

"Wait for us!" Princess Pulverizer called to Lucas. "You can't stomp out trouble by yourself!"

"You need the power of three." Dribble added. "*Us* three."

"Exactly." Princess Pulverizer picked up the pace to catch up to Lucas. "Watch out, trouble," she exclaimed. "Here we come!"

PRINCESS PULVERIZER

COLLECT EACH ADVENTURE
ON YOUR READING QUEST!

author & illustrator

nancy krulik

is the author of more than two
hundred books for children and
young adults, including three
New York Times Best Sellers.
She is the creator of several successful book
series for children, including Katie Kazoo,
Switcheroo; How I Survived Middle School;
George Brown, Class Clown; and Magic Bone.
Visit Nancy at realnancykrulik.com.

ian mcginty

is an animation director, voice
actor, and comic book artist/
writer based in Los Angeles,
California. He has worked for
Nickelodeon Studios, Marvel, BOOM! Studios,
Oni Press, and many more. Check out Ian's
work at ianmcginty.com.